this book
belongs to

First published in 2018 by Popsy & Posy Books.

ISBN: 978-1-9997913-1-5

Text copyright © Lizzie Finnigan 2018

Illustrations copyright © Katie Chappell 2018

UMBRELLA

Bella

Written by Lizzie Finnigan

Illustrated by Katie Chappell

In Purple Stone Park,
over by the waterfall,
There's an old oak tree so big and tall,
And in it lives an unusual bird called Bella
With her mummy, a rope ladder and her umbrella.

Bella thought worms were DIS-GUS-TING!!!

She preferred to dance and twirl instead of sing,
Unlike the other birds, she'd never been able to fly
- she didn't know why!

But Bella had learned to take flight with an umbrella,
So, everyone called her Umbrella Bella!

She loved flying over Purple Stone Park
Seeing the waterfall, boating pond and kids' play park,
But Bella had decided she'd like to see someplace new,
"I'm just so bored of the same old view!"

Mummy was worried about leaving Purple Stone,
Mummy warned, *"Not for long, it's risky being far from home."*

So, off they went leaving Purple Stone behind,
They didn't know where they'd end up. Bella didn't mind.
She was just excited to be seeing new things,
And was enjoying the feeling of spreading her wings.

Bella was so distracted by the new sights,
She hadn't spotted the branches in her way of flight,

Her umbrella got stuck
and ripped on the tree,
Bella crashed down,

"Uh oh! Oh dear! What's that ROARING sound I hear?"

"It's a lion! RUN! It's getting near."

Bella and Mummy needed a new plan.
Bella noticed a bird sitting on
the arm of a man,

"That bird's massive! It could
carry both you and me,
Let's ask for a birdy back
home to our tree."

"Quick, Bella!

RUN!

It's getting near!"

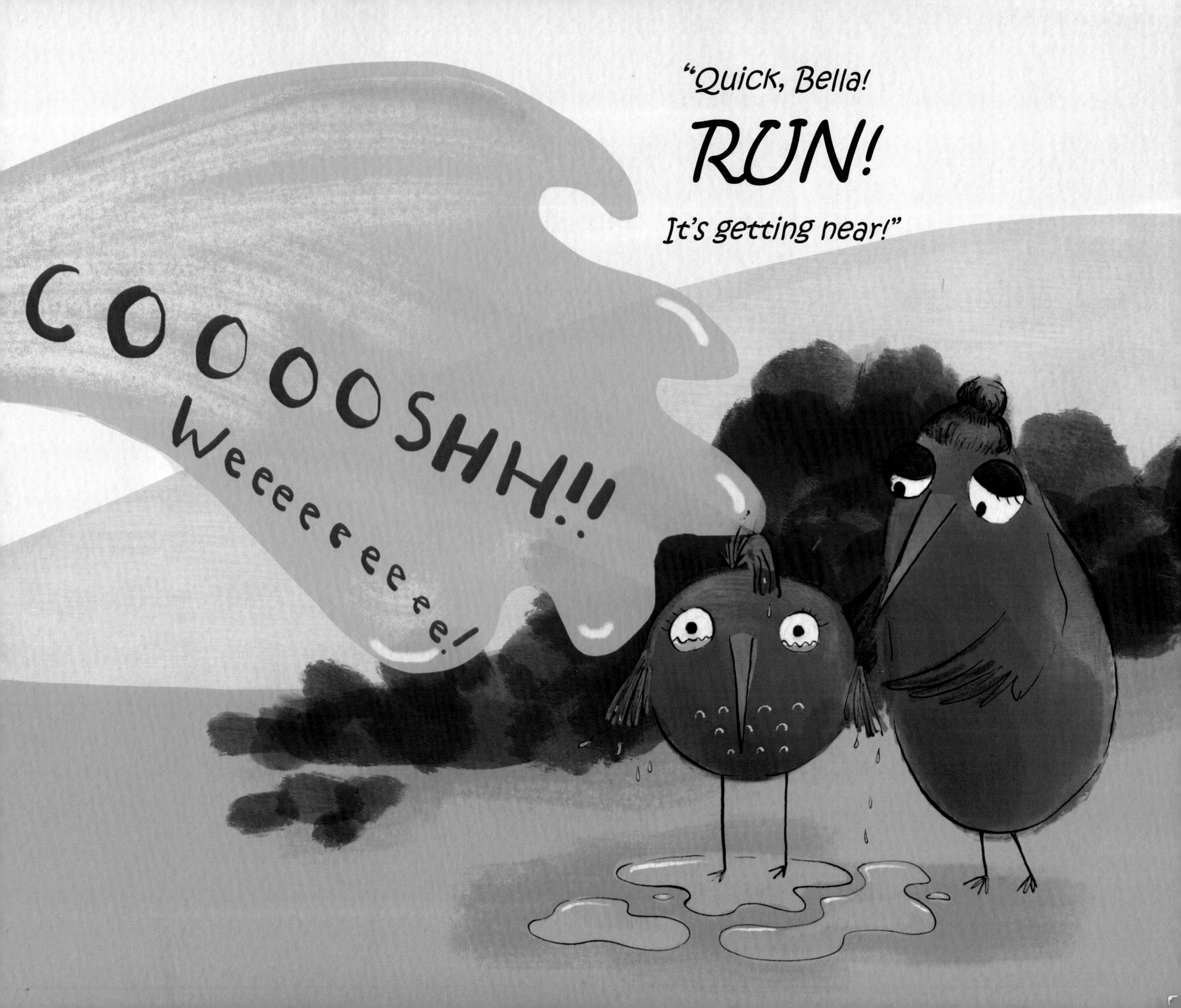

Bella was soaking wet, she was tired, she'd had enough,
Bella was in a bit of a huff!

She felt like giving up.
"It's hopeless, we'll never get back!"
Her eyes were watering,
her voice was beginning to crack.

"I miss Purple Stone - the boating pond,
the play park, the waterfall."

She couldn't hold it in and the
tears began to fall,

"Don't get upset, Bella.
I think we just both need a rest,
Let's grab a nap in that fallen nest."

Bella climbed in and snuggled under Mummy's wing,
They were sound asleep, so didn't hear a thing
The voices, the burner firing, lift off into the sky,

By the time they woke they were flying high,
Leaving the zoo they'd crashed into behind,
They were in the zoo's hot air balloon. What a lucky find!
Little did they know they'd slept in the basket of the balloon,
And it looked like they were heading the right way, they'd be home soon!

Hot air ballooning back to Purple Stone Park,
In the distance, they could see the waterfall,
the boating pond, the kids' play park,
They were getting close to their big oak tree,
"Bella, you ready? On the count of three..."

The adventure hadn't gone to plan, but Mummy and Bella still went on trips,
They were just more prepared for any umbrella rips.
They'd take a spare umbrella with them when leaving Purple Stone,
To make sure they could always make their way back home.

Home to their oak tree by Purple Stone's waterfall,
Because home was their most favourite place after all.